P9-BIR-771

Best Sisters!

Adapted by George Glass
Based on the teleplay "Giant Trouble" by Clark Stubbs
Illustrated by Steph Lew

A Random House PICTUREBACK® Book

Random House 🏠 New York

rhcbooks.com
ISBN 978-0-525-64725-6
Printed in the United States of America
10 9 8 7 6 5 4 3 2 1

One sunny day, Princess Nella and Princess Norma were enjoying a tea party in the garden behind the castle. They sat at a table with a checkered cloth, a beautiful tea set, and a big bowl of cookies.

Nella had a trick to show Norma.

"Ready?" she asked, picking up a cookie.

Princess Norma clapped and laughed.

Nella used a spoon to catapult a cookie into the air. She caught the cookie on the back of one hand and rolled it up her arm, across her shoulders, down her other arm, and into her other hand. She bit into the cookie with a chomp!

Norma giggled and waved her hands with delight.

Hearing the laughter, Trinket trotted over to the sisters.
"Are you guys tea-partying? she asked.
"We're having a best-sisters playdate!" Nella replied.
"Care for a spot of lemonade?"
But before Nella could serve Trinket, a giant snowball
flew out of the sky and landed on her best unicorn friend!

"What is this?" Trinket cried, leaping from the pile of cold mush.

"Snow!" Nella said with surprise.

"But how can it be snowing?" Trinket asked. "There's not a cloud in the sky!"

"Come on, Norma," said Nella. "We've got to get you inside." She picked up her little sister and carried her into the house.

Just then, Sir Garrett and Clod came rushing over.
"Nella! Trinket!" said Sir Garrett. "There are giant snowballs flying all over the kingdom!"

"This snowstorm is ruining Nella and Norma's tea party," Trinket lamented.

Suddenly, a strange voice echoed from far away: "I'll show you!"

Nella and her friends looked at the two mountains in the distance. They saw a huge creature on top of each peak.

"Those are the Rock Giants!" Sir Garrett announced, pulling out his Knightly Trading Cards. "It says right here that they're made out of big rocks, and they're practically as big as mountains."

"Well, they're making a big mess!" said Nella. "And I've got to do something about it," said Nella. "My heart is shining bright—time to be a Princess Knight!" Nella's transformed into a Princess Knight. Then she and Trinket rode to one peak while Sir Garrett and Clod galloped to the other one.

On one snowy mountain, Nella and Trinket
met a Rock Giant named Trevor. Nella realized
Trevor wasn't throwing snow at Castlehaven.
He was throwing it at his little brother, Grud,
who was on the other mountain.

"He's such a pain," Trevor grumbled. "Always
coming to my room, always taking my things!"
He went back to throwing snowballs.

"Brothers aren't supposed to fight," said Nella.
She had an idea to help them get along. "If you're
tired of throwing snowballs at your brother, you could
always come over to the castle for a tea party. With
lots of pretty cups, and lemonade, and cookies . . ."

"Did you say cookies?" Trevor asked excitedly.
"Cookies are my favorite! I'd love to come."

Nella transformed her sword into a bow and shot a ribbon arrow with an invitation on it. The arrow sailed all the way to the other peak, where Sir Garrett caught it.

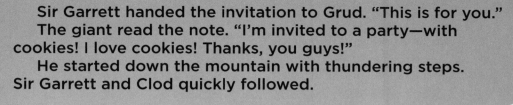

Sir Garrett handed the invitation to Grud. "This is for you."

The giant read the note. "I'm invited to a party—with cookies! I love cookies! Thanks, you guys!"

He started down the mountain with thundering steps. Sir Garrett and Clod quickly followed.

Later, Nella was back at the castle preparing for the tea party. There was still snow all over the garden.

"Good thing we had a lot of leftover cookie dough," she said, grunting as she set a big bowl of giant cookies on the table. She looked at her little sister. "Ready to try this playdate one more time?"

Sir Garrett and Clod arrived first with their guest from the mountain.

"Please join our tea party," said Nella, welcoming Grud. "Have a seat."

Grud tried to sit on a chair, but he crushed it with his massive weight.

"Don't worry about that," Nella said, handing him a teacup. "You can just sit on the grass."

Then everyone heard booming footsteps.
"I wonder who that could be," Nella said in a singsong voice.
It was Trevor!
The two brothers glared at each other and said, "What's *he* doing here?"
The giants scooped up snowballs and got ready to fight.

Nella stood between the giants. "Let's all stay calm and play nice."

Trevor threw the first snowball. It went way past Grud and hit a tower on the castle.

"Ha! Missed me!" mocked Grud. He threw his snowball and hit a nearby house.

"Dragon burps!" Sir Garrett exclaimed as another giant snowball rolled into him. "This is getting out of hand!"

"Stop throwing snowballs at me, Trevor!" warned Grud.

"No, *you* stop throwing snowballs at *me,* Grud!" Trevor replied.

Norma started to whimper in her high chair.

"Guys, guys!" shouted Nella. "You're brothers! You've got to start getting along. And you're upsetting Norma."

Nella knew how to calm her sister. She bounced a small cookie into the air with a spoon, rolled it along one arm and then the other, and popped it into her mouth.
Norma laughed happily.

Nella grabbed a giant cookie from the large bowl. "Hey, Trevor! Grud!" she said. "You like cookies, right?"

"Yeah, we love cookies!" answered Trevor.

"Both of us!" added Grud.

Trevor and Grud watched the sisters laughing together. "Too bad we don't have a giant spoon," said Trevor, "so we could do what you and Princess Norma were doing."

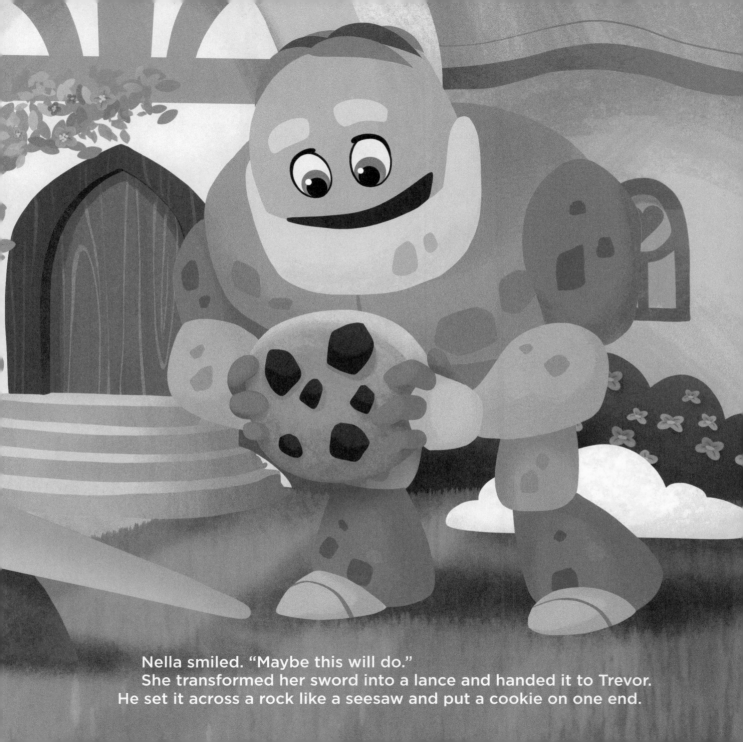

Nella smiled. "Maybe this will do."
She transformed her sword into a lance and handed it to Trevor.
He set it across a rock like a seesaw and put a cookie on one end.

"Here you go, little bro," Trevor said as he swatted the handle of the lance. The cookie popped into the air.

Grud caught the cookie, ate it happily in one bite, and yelled, "Again!"

Trevor launched another cookie—even higher this time. Grud jumped into the air, caught the cookie behind his back, and tossed it into his mouth with a loud crunch.

"These brothers are great together!" said Clod.
Nella looked around happily. "Now, *this* is a tea party."
Trevor smiled at his little brother. "You know, you can be kind of fun, little bro."
Grud smiled back at his big brother. "You too, big bro."
Norma looked up at her big sister and cooed happily.

"I couldn't agree more, Norma," said Nella as she reached down and hugged her little sister.

The best sisters—and the best brothers—enjoyed the rest of the tea party with their best friends!